When Uncle Jim moved to the city, he gave his dog, Rasty, to Christopher. Christopher was ready to like Rasty, but Rasty did not like Christopher. As a matter of fact, he didn't like anyone who came to Christopher's house and pretty soon no one came.

"You must get rid of Rasty," said Christopher's parents. But how?

Read about Christopher's trouble and find out how Rasty himself helped to solve the problem.

The TERRIBLE TERRIER

By EDITH BATTLES

Pictures by TOM FUNK

YOUNG SCOTT BOOKS

RASTY

1655936

When Uncle Jim moved to the city, he gave Christopher his dog. Christopher liked Rasty, but he wasn't so sure Rasty liked him.

Christopher's father liked Rasty, but
Rasty did not like Christopher's
father.

Christopher's mother wasn't so sure she liked Rasty,
but Rasty was *very* sure he did not like her.

Rasty did not like the garbage man, either. Rasty
did not want him to take away the trash. He
guarded the bags very carefully.

Rasty did not like the mailman. He growled whenever the mailman put strange white papers through the slot in the door. Every day he tried to snatch the postman's fingers.

Rasty did not like the paper boy who tossed the newspaper on the lawn each day. Rasty did not like litter.

Rasty did not like the electric meter man who wanted to get into the cellar.

One day the garbage man did not
collect the trash.
The paper boy stopped delivering papers.
The mailman stopped delivering mail. And
the meter man sent a notice to keep the dog
tied up or start using candles.

"There must be someone Rasty likes,"
said Christopher's mother.
"But will that someone like Rasty?"
asked Christopher's father.
"Maybe someone will like him if I
give him away free with ten cans of
dog food," said Christopher. "Every-
body on our street likes dogs a little.
Except Mr. Grumps. He doesn't like
anybody."

Christopher put a leash on Rasty and dragged him down the street. His first stop was at Dr. Bell's house.

Dr. Bell opened the door. Rasty growled. "I treat people," said Dr. Bell. "I am not a vet."

"He isn't sick. I am giving him away."

"No thanks," said Dr. Bell. "He would be good for business, but I would soon run out of bandages. Good-bye."

Rasty growled all the way to Mrs. Means's house.

"That's the creature!" yelled Mrs. Means when she saw Rasty. "That's the dog that scared my poor kitty up onto the roof. Go away, dog. Scat!"

"Please wag your tail a little," coaxed Christopher. "Then maybe the dentist will like you." But Rasty just opened his mouth and showed a lot of teeth.

The dentist opened the door and then quickly closed it to a crack.
"I never look into a mouth that is big enough to swallow me."

Next door, Mr. Murphy's dog was watching from the window. Rasty yanked Christopher up the steps. Rasty and Mr. Murphy's dog called each other names through the window glass.

"How can I find a home for you if you don't even like dogs!"

Christopher was surprised at how many people
Rasty knew. Whenever they saw him coming, they
ran inside and slammed their doors.

Amelia and her friends were gathered at the ice-cream truck. Rasty raced toward them.
"BOW-WOW-RRF!" he roared.
The ice-cream man dropped his box of ice-cream bars. Amelia fell down and her ice cream got dirty.
Rasty raced on, pulling Christopher after him.

Rasty dragged Christopher past old Mr. Grumps.
No use even asking him, thought Christopher. He
never lets anyone pick apples from his trees or take
a short cut across his lawn.

Suddenly Rasty saw Mr. Grumps picking apples. He began to wag his tail. Then he pulled so hard on the leash that Christopher had to let go. Rasty ran over to Mr. Grumps with his tail still wagging.

When Christopher tried to go on Mr. Grumps's lawn to get Rasty, Rasty growled at him.

"Hey, boy, get off my lawn," said Mr. Grumps.

"Yes, sir," said Christopher. "But what about Rasty?" Rasty growled at Christopher again.

"I need a good watchdog," said Mr. Grumps. "And this dog suits me fine. What do you want for him?"

"He's free," said Christopher. "Good-bye, Rasty." Rasty growled good-bye.

"Well," said Christopher when he got home, "Rasty is going to be very busy guarding Mr. Grumps's house, and I'm going to be very busy looking for another pet."

"How about a hamster?"
asked Christopher's mother.